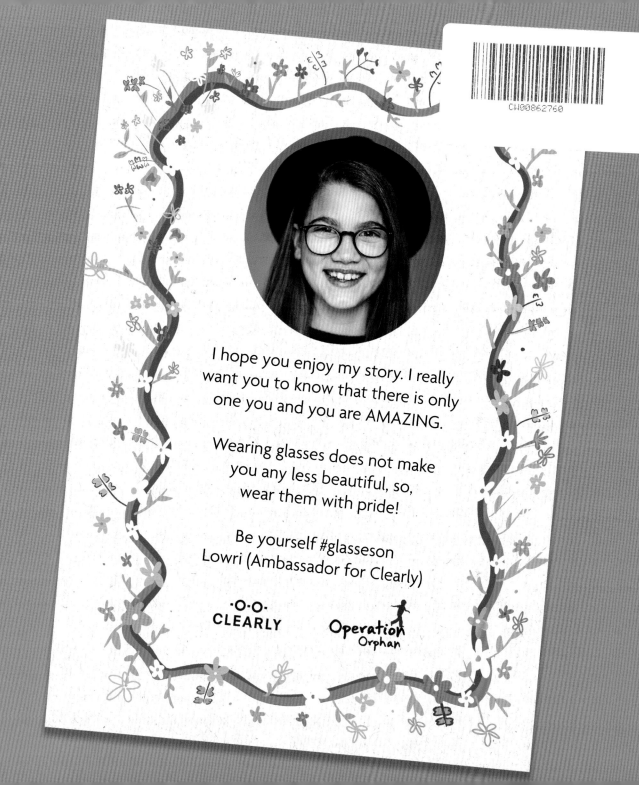

I hope you enjoy my story. I really want you to know that there is only one you and you are AMAZING.

Wearing glasses does not make you any less beautiful, so, wear them with pride!

Be yourself #glasseson
Lowri (Ambassador for Clearly)

·O·O·
CLEARLY

Operation
Orphan

The autumn leaves had begun to fall in the kingdom, and young Princess Rose was given a special gift from the king and queen.

"Here you go Rose, your new pair of glasses," her
mother, Queen Cyrilyn, said with a smile.

Princess Rose looked down at the glasses. Sparkles
shone from the frames and the glass reflected the
sunlight coming in from the window.

"Thank you mother," Rose said, taking the glasses
from her. As soon as her mother left the room,
Rose's smile quickly turned to sadness and
she flopped down onto the floor.

"How can you be a princess if you wear glasses?" a dark voice said from across the room.

"Who said that?" Rose asked, startled.

"Who said what?" a friendly-sounding voice asked.

Her friends Prince Omar and the Princesses Violet and Scarlett had arrived at the palace for afternoon tea.

They sat down with King Bradley and Queen Cyrilyn at the grand
table. Whilst helping themselves to the beautiful cakes
and scones, the dark voice that Rose had heard in her
room suddenly reappeared.

"You see those princesses across the table?
They aren't wearing glasses."

Rose tried to ignore the voice as
she tucked into her slice of cake.
But the voice kept getting louder and louder.

Rose gasped in disbelief as a ghostly
version of herself appeared right in front of her.
It slithered onto the seat next to her.

"Shhhhh," it said to Rose, "I am Angusina.
Nobody else can see or hear me, only you."

Rose closed her eyes, hoping that Angusina would go away. When she opened her eyes again, the ghostly figure was still sitting next to her.

"They aren't wearing glasses because they are real princesses, you aren't a princess, you will never fit in with them!" Angusina cackled.

Rose's eyes filled with tears. "Just stop it! Go away!" she shouted, putting her hands over her face.

Everyone in the room stopped what they were doing and stared. "Sweetheart, are you ok?" the queen asked.

Rose looked up from her hands. Her face felt like it was burning, and with embarrassment, she ran out of the room.

"Whatever was that all about?" the king asked.

"I think I have an idea," replied the queen, rising to her feet. "Omar, Scarlett and Violet, I need your help, come with me." And with that, they all followed the queen.

As for Rose, she kept running. She ran out of the kingdom. She ran until her legs simply couldn't run anymore. She ran all the way to the beach. The waves crashed against the sand as she stood beside the water. Salty tears ran down her cheeks as she tried to catch her breath.

"You are all alone now," said Angusina.

Rose looked up, her eyes filled with tears.

"Why are you being so mean? How can I be a real princess? I can't even see without my glasses," Rose sobbed, quietly taking off her glasses to reveal a blurry sunset in the distance.

"That's because you aren't a real princess, how can you be when you wear glasses?" smirked Angusina.

Rose threw a rock at the ghostly figure. It went straight through her and into the sea, making Angusina disappear.

In place of the rock floated a little bottle. Rose sniffed back her tears as she picked up the mysterious bottle. Inside was this message...

'Princess Rose, follow the clues to find the answers to all of your questions. The clues will look familiar to you.' Rose looked puzzled.

"The answer to my questions? Maybe it will tell me if I am a real princess or not," Rose said to herself.

"Or it will tell you that you aren't a princess. Think about it, none of your family wear glasses so how can you possibly be a princess?" the dark voice echoed around her.

Rose shut her eyes tight. When she re-opened them she noticed something glittering beneath the sand, near to where she stood. Rose pulled a long necklace from the sand. It had a sea shell attached to it. She turned it over and saw a message.

'Don't allow bad thoughts to take you over. Follow the sea shore until you get to the frozen water.'

DON'T ALLOW BAD THOUGHTS TO TAKE YOU OVER. FOLLOW THE SEA SHORE UNTIL YOU GET TO THE FROZEN WATER

Rose skipped along the edge of the water, leaving the sun and sand behind her. She kept going until she skidded onto a patch of ice - she had at last reached the frozen water!

FIND THE BOW
AND ARROW

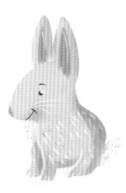

Snowflakes began to fall around her like a winter wonderland.

Rose looked down at the floor and spotted footprints in the snow. She scratched her head and wondered whose they could be.

Underneath a tall tree stood a snowman. Rose ran over towards it, could this be the next clue?

A note hung around the snowman's neck. It read:
'Find the bow and arrow.'

"What's the point in trying Rose? The only answers you will find will be disappointing." Angusina shouted, startling her.

Trying not to pay attention to Angusina, Rose continued her journey towards the next clue. As she left the icy weather behind her, she stumbled upon a long, winding path.

Rose began to feel calmer as she kicked through the leaves along the path.
Her long hair blew in the wind. She began to scan the area for the next clue.

Suddenly, something shiny caught her eye. Hidden in the grass was a bow and arrow with
a long piece of rope attached. Bewildered, but thrilled to find the next clue, Rose picked it
up, feeling the cold, sharp metal through her fingers.

Scratched into the surface of the arrow read,
'Find the enchanted staircase.'

FIND THE
ENCHANTED STAIRCASE

"Hmm, I wonder why it has a rope attached to it?" Rose thought to herself,
when suddenly the ground began to fall from beneath her feet.
Rose screamed in panic as she fell down into an enormous black hole.

She'd never used a bow and arrow before.
Pulling back the bow, she released the arrow upwards.
The arrow flew into the sky and with a loud snap,
it lodged itself into a nearby tree.
Rose pulled hard on the rope to save herself from falling any further.

"Well, that's it, you are done for!"
shouted Angusina from the top of the hole.

"No I am not!"
Rose shouted back as she began to pull with all her might on the rope.

Feeling exhausted, Rose managed to climb to the top of
the hole by pulling herself up.

She fell backwards onto the soft grass, trying to get her breath back.
As she glanced to the side of her, she noticed another path.
Rose stood to her feet and began to follow it.

Further along in the distance she could see what
looked like an old palace. As she arrived at the
palace doors, she saw how old it was. The sparkle
had definitely disappeared from this palace.
It was not a place Rose had ever seen before.

She quickly ran up the steps toward the doorway.
As she made her way up the steps, she noticed a
familiar looking slipper made of glass.

Could this be the next clue? Were these the
steps of the enchanted staircase that had been
written about on the last clue?

As Rose looked more closely at the slipper, she noticed a note pushed inside. The note read, 'It is the courage to continue that counts. Find your next clue in the blue book.'

Angusina was sitting on the side of the steps.

"You do know you won't make it to the end of this little adventure, don't you? You will fail to find all of the clues," she hissed.

Rose pushed past her and entered through the gigantic doors.

What would have once been a glittering hallway, was now an empty room.

As Rose walked around she could hear the echo of her footsteps. Each room she entered was empty. She ran around until she reached the ballroom. She could imagine the men and women dancing in this gigantic room.

Rose spun around, dancing to the music in her mind. As she spun and spun, she tripped over something in the middle of the floor.

Rose bent down and picked it up. It was the blue book. Inside was a beautiful rose that stuck out from the pages, it revealed a note written on the page, saying, 'Find your last clue within the dark forest.'

Rose held the book tightly as she looked through the tall glass window towards a dark forest. She looked around to find her way out and found an open door in the ballroom.

FIND YOUR LAST CLUE WITHIN THE DARK FOREST

Droplets of rain began to fall as she stepped through the doors.
As she ran through the puddles, who should appear right in
front of her, but Angusina.

"Just stop! You wear glasses so even if you do reach the end,
you still will never be a princess!" hissed Angusina.

Rose pulled off her glasses in rage.
"You are right, I'm not a real princess if I wear glasses."

Rose shoved her glasses into her pocket, and continued to head
towards the dark forest. She had one last clue to find - but could
she do it without her glasses?

Rose stretched out her arms, she couldn't see a single thing in front
of her. The darkness surrounded her. "Ouch!" screamed Rose, as her
hands scraped against the thorns along the branches around her.
Determined to get to where she needed to be, Rose pushed past
the trees, gritting her teeth.

"You foolish girl, you are blind to the world,"
Angusina snarled at Rose.

Rose began to cry as she fumbled around, trying to find something to
hold onto. The wet mud slipped beneath her feet and she fell down
the side of the muddy bank. Rose's glasses had fallen out of her
pocket as she fell.

"Where have they gone?!" Rose cried as she put her hands out onto
the floor, desperately trying to find them.

CRUNCH!

She felt the cracked lens of the glasses underneath her foot. Sadly Rose put her broken glasses back on and sniffed back her tears. She thought she could have found the final clue without her glasses, but she was wrong.

"Angusina was right! I'm not a princess, I don't have courage, I'm not brave, I don't have a prince to save me, and I am not beautiful. I will never reach the final clue!"

At that moment, an apple rolled right towards her feet.

Rose looked at the apple and noticed a note attached to it with a piece of string. The note said, 'Find the cottage at the top of the hill.'

Rose looked ahead of her and spotted a hill. "The cottage must be at the top of that," she told herself.

Rose jumped to her feet.

"Don't bother going, you won't find the cottage."
Angusina appeared once again next to Rose.
This time, Rose ignored the voice and began to run towards the hill.
With each step she took Angusina shouted, "Stop! You won't find what
you are looking for in the cottage. You are not a princess."

More determined than ever, Rose reached the top of the hill
to find on top of it was a small cottage surrounded by beautiful flowers.

Angusina sprung from behind a tree.
"You are not worthy to go in there, you aren't a princess."

Rose stopped and looked straight at Angusina. "Maybe you are
right, but I need to find out what's in the cottage. I have come
this far," she said. And with that, she opened the door.

Rose stepped into a room, empty except for a portrait on the table. Cobwebs and dust covered the image that lay beneath.

"See, there is nothing in here for you," Angusina whispered to Rose. Rose began to brush the dust away from the image, then stood back to have a better view.

The picture on the wall showed a beautiful lady in a vibrant orange dress, wearing a royal tiara and... glasses.

Looking down at the table, Rose spotted a box. She opened the box gently, uncovering a beautiful pair of glistening, golden glasses.

The very same glasses that were on the painting in front of her.

"See... not even an answer to your question,"
Angusina laughed. "You are nothing!"

Rose began to smile. Angusina's face dropped.
"What are you smiling about? You should be crying!"

Rose turned to Angusina and read from a note in the box: "You are beautiful, no matter what."

Angusina fell back in disbelief.

"This means I am a princess! I am beautiful, I am brave, I do have courage and I don't need you following me around giving me bad thoughts any more," Rose said confidently.

Angusina screamed out in agony. A dark cloud burst around Rose, and a bright light shone in front of her. She had done it, she had overcome her dark thoughts.

"You were named after your Grandmother," a friendly voice said behind her.

Rose spun around to see Queen Cyrilyn, King Bradley, Prince Omar, and Princesses Violet and Scarlett together in the doorway.

"I know you don't remember your Grandmother, but she knew you when you were only a little girl. She sadly isn't with us anymore but she loved you very much. She would be so proud of you," Rose's mother replied.

"When I was little I had troubles with my demons,
and they would tell me horrible things that I would believe.
Grandmother Rose was a queen who never gave in to her demons.
She was wise and helped me to realise that I was beautiful,
and that I was a brave young woman."

Rose hugged her mother.

"Thank you for showing me that I too am beautiful within,
but how did the clues appear?" asked Rose.

"All of us, including your friends, hid the clues to help you follow your own path in
realising the answer that you knew deep down all along:
that you are beautiful no matter what," said Queen Cyrilyn.

Rose's eyes filled with happy tears.
She looked over at her friends, who smiled back.

"We all want you to know that you are worthy of being a princess! You have a
heart of gold, we all love you and want you to be happy," smiled Prince Omar.

"Here, Queen Rose would have wanted you to have these,"
smiled her father as he handed Rose the golden glasses from the box.

"I'll make Grandmother proud of the confident girl I have become."

Rose smiled as she put on her beautiful new glasses. Rose could finally see that
with a good heart, courage, and kindness, true beauty lies within.